Luba AND THE Wren

For children everywhere,
who should be full of joy and
free from care

---

*"For where your treasure is,
there will your heart be also"*

Matthew 6:21

ISBN 0-439-23880-3

Copyright © 1999 by Patricia Polacco. All rights reserved.
Published by Scholastic Inc., 555 Broadway, New York, NY 10012, by arrangement with Philomel Books, a division of Penguin Putnam, Inc.
SCHOLASTIC and associated logos are trademarks and/or registered trademarks of Scholastic Inc.

12 11 10 9 8 7 6 5 4 3 2   0 1 2 3 4 5/0

Printed in the U.S.A.   14

First Scholastic printing, September 2000

Book design by Donna Mark
The text is set in Galliard.

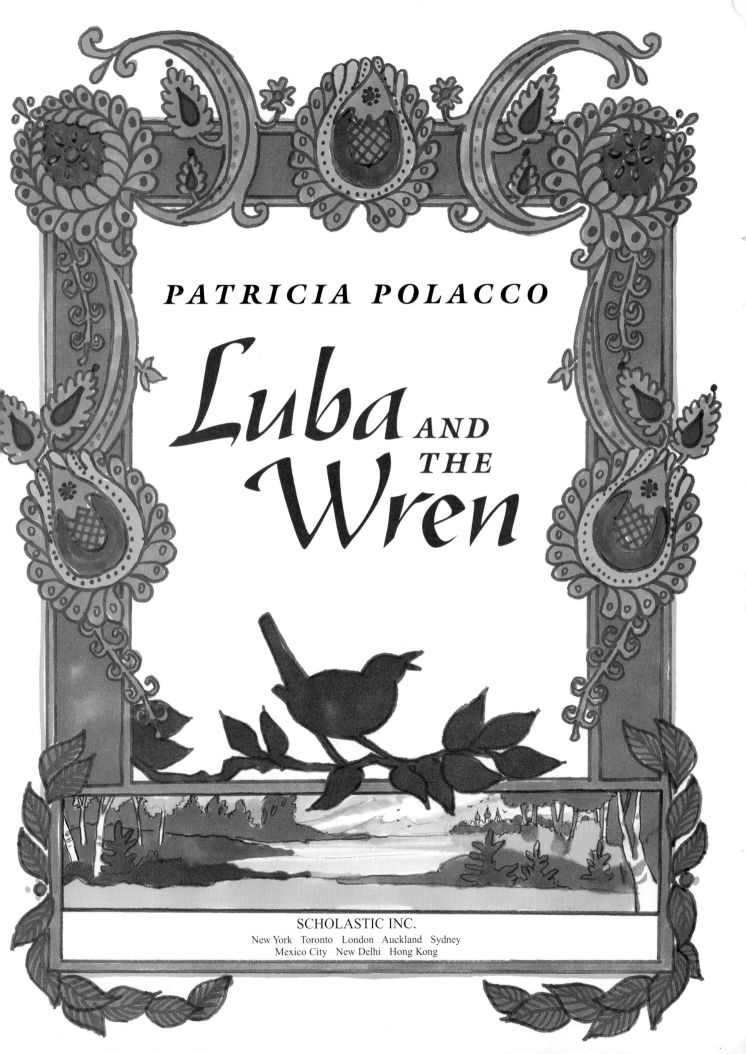

PATRICIA POLACCO

Luba AND THE Wren

SCHOLASTIC INC.

New York   Toronto   London   Auckland   Sydney
Mexico City   New Delhi   Hong Kong

Once there was a poor farmer and his wife. They lived with their only child, Luba, in a humble dacha in a clearing on the edge of a deep forest.

Their house was crowded and small. The roof leaked. The fences needed mending. The fields, although lovingly tended, were meager and bare. They had little comfort. But their daughter, Luba, was full of joy and free from care as all children should be.

One day, as Luba was looking for mushrooms deep in the forest, she heard a small pitiful cry coming from the tree above her. There she saw the most beautiful, delicate little wren caught in a fowler's net. She took pity on this little creature and climbed the tree to free it. It took wing and sang a glorious song, then it fluttered down from the sky and landed on a branch next to her. To Luba's astonishment, the little bird spoke.

"My dear, how can I ever repay you for saving my life?" it asked.

When Luba found her voice, she replied. "I would have done the same for any creature, little one."

"For your kindness," the bird said, "I shall grant you any wish that you may ask of me, for I am enchanted."

"But I am content, I have no wish," Luba said as she shyly laughed.

"If ever you want for anything, come to the forest and call me," the bird said.

Luba ran all the way home and burst into the house and told her mother and father about the enchanted wren.

"Foolish girl!" her mother groaned. "Why didn't you ask the wren for a bigger house!"

"You know how hard life is for us….We are so poor!" her father said.

"Couldn't you go back and ask?" her mother said wearily.

"Go back to the forest and ask the wren for a bigger house on fertile land," they both pleaded.

Luba did as they asked and went to the edge of the forest.

"Little wren, little wren…please come to me," she sang out.

"Dear one," the wren chirped as she landed on a tree branch above Luba, "what is it you wish?"

"It is not mine," Luba said shyly. "It is my parents' wish that brings me back to you."

"What, then, do they want?" the wren asked cheerfully.

"A bigger house! They would like to have more room and also to have land that is rich and fertile so they don't have to work so hard to grow things."

"Go then, dear one," the wren said. "For it is already done!"

Sure enough, as Luba got to the clearing where her small dacha had been, there stood a grand farmhouse indeed. Her parents greeted her. Their clothes were new and not patched. Their land was lush and fertile. The orchards were full of trees heavy with ripe fruit.

Luba's heart sang. She knew that her parents would be happy and content.

But, alas, within weeks they were pacing the floor.

"We have been thinking," they said as they paced, "we would like to have a bigger house, with more fields and workers to help us farm!"

"But I have already asked the wren for this wonderful farm. How can I ask her for more?" said Luba.

"You saved her life," her father said sternly. "She owes this wish to you!"

"Now go and ask the wren for a manor house with acres and acres of land!" her mother ordered.

Luba went to the edge of the forest. She was reluctant to call the little wren, but the wren came as soon as she heard Luba's voice.

"Dear one, what is it now?" the wren asked.

"It is not for me, and I wouldn't ask again, but it is my parents. They no longer like the farmhouse. Now they want an estate with acres of land, and servants."

The wren could see that the child was ashamed.
"Go then, my dear," the wren said. "For it is
already done!"

When Luba returned home, there, instead of a
big farmhouse, stood a graceful house of estate
surrounded by lush gardens, ponds and honking
geese, and swans.

As she entered the house, her father was seated by the fireplace in a grand chair. He was truly Lord of the Manor. Her mother was seated next to him, being tended by handmaidens. Spread before them was a great table glowing with all kinds of wondrous things to eat. Now Luba was sure they would be happy and content.

But just as before, Luba awoke one morning to see her parents pacing the floor. "We have been thinking," they began. "Since the wren can grant us anything we want, why didn't we ask for a palace in the first place?"

"But Mama, Papa," Luba pleaded, "I cannot ask the wren again!"

"Ah, but you can!" the father hissed. "After all, you saved her life, didn't you?"

"She should be grateful!" her mother bellowed.

"Go now!" they ordered. "And not only do we want a palace, but we wish to be rulers of all the Ukraine!"

Luba walked slowly to the edge of the forest. Her heart was heavy. The sky was gray and dark. The forest looked bleak and unfriendly. Luba called for the wren. The wren came.

"What is it they wish now?" the wren asked sternly.

"Now they want to live in a palace and be rulers of all the Ukraine!" Luba answered, barely able to speak.

"Go then, my child," the wren said. "It is already done!"

When Luba arrived home, she stood in the courtyard of a majestic palace. Everywhere she looked there were uniformed servants and guards. When she entered the palace, there were her parents, surrounded by chancellors and vice chancellors and noblemen from all the counties and estates in the Ukraine.

I hope that this makes them happy at last! Luba thought.

And they were, for a time. But then one morning Luba awoke to find her parents standing near her bed.

"We have been thinking," they said. "Being rulers of the Ukraine is not what we thought it would be. Go to the wren and ask her to make us the Tzar and Tzarina of all the Russias!"

"This I cannot do!" Luba cried.

"You must!" they said. "After all, we are the rulers of the Ukraine, and you must not disobey!"

When Luba got to the forest, the wren was waiting for her! The sky was full of billowing clouds, gray and stormy. Lightning crackled at their edges.

"Now what do they want?" the wren asked impatiently.

"They want to be the Tzar and Tzarina of all the Russias," Luba answered as she sobbed.

"Go then, it is already done!" the wren sighed.

As Luba approached the clearing, she saw the onion domes of the Tzars gleaming in the sun. Then she saw her parents, the Tzar and Tzarina of all the Russias, drive up in a golden coach, festooned with riches and splendor that she had never imagined in her life.

Surely, she thought to herself, this will finally make them happy and content.

This time it seemed that, at long last, they finally were. Then one day Luba found them pacing the Great Hall. As Luba approached them, they said, "Ah, Luba…we were thinking, now that we are Tzar and Tzarina of all the Russias, we see absolutely no reason why we cannot be Emperor and Empress of the entire world!"

Luba could not speak.

"Go to the wren and make this so, we command you!" they growled.

Luba hardly recognized her parents anymore. But she did as they asked.

When she entered the forest this day, the sky was blacker
than black. The trees twisted harshly. Storm clouds rolled angrily
in the sky. The wind seemed to push against her every step. The
wren was waiting for her.

"What now?" the wren snapped.

Luba did not speak for the longest time, but finally she found
the words.

"They wish to be Emperor and Empress of all the world!"

"Go then," the wren said. "It is already done."

Luba stood in the majestic throne room. There, seated on the tallest thrones, were her parents, Emperor and Empress of all the world! They didn't even speak to her. Leaders from all lands near and far were bowing at their feet.

At long last! Luba thought. They are happy and content.

Then, one day, as all the times before, she saw her parents standing, looking out of the window of her room.

"We have been thinking," they hissed. "We want more… much, much, much more! We want to be as Gods!"

Luba was stunned. "No Papa…Mama! Do you hear what you are saying? This is sacrilege!"

"Silence!" they thundered. "Go ask the wren!"

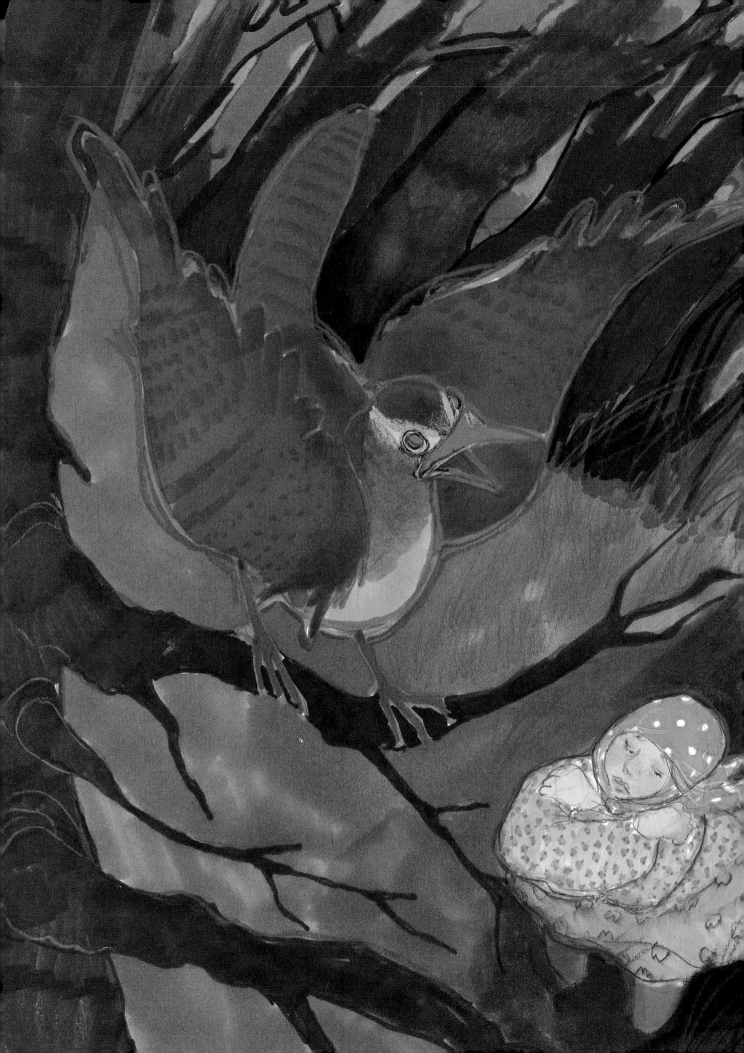

Luba went to the forest. Never had the journey taken so long. A fierce storm raged in the sky above her. The wind howled, the trees writhed and shook. But the wren was waiting. Luba could not find the words to ask this wish! She just stood and cried.

"And now?" the wren asked almost sadly.

"They…want to be as…Gods!" Luba choked through her tears.

Lightning slashed the sky in half. The thunder cried out Luba's name; the ground pitched and buckled under her feet.

"Go then, my child," the wren said softly. "It is already done!"

Luba walked sadly back to the clearing. Her steps were heavy, her heart ached. But as she reached the clearing…

She was astonished to see her little dacha! That dear little house just as it was before. The fences needed mending; the roof leaked; the fields were meager and bare.

Then she saw her mama and papa sitting on the front porch. Her mother was mending torn clothing. Her father was carving a small piece of wood.

"Here is our dear treasure now!" her mother exclaimed.

"I made this today just for you," her father said as he showed her a carving of a small wooden bird.

"Was it wonderful in the forest today?" they said as they stretched out their arms to her.

Luba leaped into their warm embrace.

At long last, her parents were happy, and very, very content indeed.